CW00793613

WRECKED

ABBY KNOX

Copyright © 2022 by Abby Knox

All rights reserved.

No part of this book may be reproduced in any form or by any electronic or mechanical means, including information storage and retrieval systems, without written permission from the author, except for the use of brief quotations in a book review.

Publisher's Note: This is a work of fiction. Names, characters, places, and incidents are a product of the author's imagination. Locales and public names are sometimes used for atmospheric purposes. Any resemblance to actual people, living or dead, or to businesses, companies, events, institutions, or locales is coincidental.

Edited by Aquila Editing

Cover Designer: Cormar Covers

❀ Created with Vellum

Summary

Juno

Now that I've been promoted to chief steward on the yacht Carpe Diem, I have to at least try to get along with our tempestuous chef. Yet, Maksim and I can't seem to play nice. Something about him makes my claws come out, and whenever we are together in the galley, it's more than his cooking that's aflame. My feelings might be hurt at the way we trade barbs, if he weren't such an egotistical hothead. Me? I'll just keep doing what I do best: say yes to the guests and never back down from a challenge. Even if that challenge is a glowering, towering man with eyes that seem to see right through me.

Maksim

I did not join this crew to get attached to a woman; I came here to start a new life. Even if my innermost feelings demand something more than a solitary existence. I'll just have to deal with it; anyone attached to me will only end up with a target on her back, same as me. Leaving behind my job as a hired assassin doesn't mean I deserve any kind of normal, homey type of life. And yet, Juno is in my head. The smart-mouthed chief stew can't seem to stay in her lane, stay out of my galley, or stay out of my dreams. When we try to work together, all we do is trade barbs. I wouldn't care about the banter, but I'm enjoying it too much. The more I push her away the more my body and soul find ways to be close to her. Maybe a yacht wasn't the best choice if I want to avoid connecting with other people. Maybe a hot kitchen, with a hotter chief stew constantly buzzing around me, is too much for my cold heart.

Naughty Yachties is a new series of short romance stories loosely inspired by Below Deck. If you love romance tropes, obsessed heroes, plucky heroines, high heat, and happily ever afters, then welcome aboard!

Chapter One

Maksim

THE ONLY WAY out of the underworld is to disappear or live as an always-moving target.

I'm doing both and hoping for the best.

I spent a small fortune on Dmitri, who sold me a new identity. I threw in a lot extra for him to start the rumor that I was killed by accidentally ingesting my own poison that I've used on many of my victims.

As soon as I landed in Monte Carlo, I spent another fortune on new chef's knives—adding another layer to my new identity. I do know my knives. These blades will only be assassinating shellfish, and I can't wait to get started.

Today, I'm standing in the galley of the superyacht Carpe Diem in the Mediterranean off the coast of Naples. The provision sheet in front of me describes the wants and needs of some wealthy American influencer who doesn't know the difference between excellent caviar and caviar that tastes as if scraped from the bottom of this boat.

"Problem?"

The question comes from the stewardess who plagues me night and day.

With the departure of Vanessa, Juno has been moved up to chief stew. So now, she's buzzing around me night and day. She loves to tell me how to plate my food, how to order ingredients, and sometimes, even how to cook it.

One small blessing is she doesn't smile at me; she saves that for the guests.

The rest of the crew? Too nice. All of them smile all the time, and it makes me paranoid.

Juno doesn't give a shit. Especially about my moods or whether or not I'm having a "nice day." Like right now, she can see how agitated I am, and she just keeps poking.

"Yes, I have a problem. I'm not ordering this," I tell her, pointing to the cheap caviar listed on the provision sheet.

She laughs. God, that laugh. The sound bothers my ears like a chittering chipmunk. It might be cute if she weren't such a busy bee in my face…in my thoughts…in my dreams.

"That's what the primary wants; that's what the primary gets." She folds her arms as if that's the end of the argument.

"She has terrible taste," I retort.

Juno rolls her eyes. "Most of them do. We are not here to judge. We are here to give them what they want."

I want to tell Juno that her previous boss, Vanessa, would have been able to finesse the primary. But for some reason, I don't want to hurt her feelings. Weird, because she seems like she's made of steel sometimes.

"This is the kind I ordered." I show her the receipt from the provisioners. "And it is better. They will taste it, and they will agree."

Juno's confident expression falters a bit. "Maksim. You and I have to work together as a team now. Do you understand that?"

I nod tersely. "I understand English perfectly. Better than most of the people on this crew."

"Rude," she says.

"I didn't mean you," I growl.

Juno smirks. "Oh yeah? Is that you paying me a compliment? Because I might just faint, big guy."

A strange thing happens when she calls me "big guy." I feel like someone has dropped a pebble into my stomach. A hot stone, causing a ripple of sensation out to my limbs. I do not like this feeling. It surges like someone caressing me from the inside out.

Probably the beginnings of a stomach virus.

"Why are you looking at me like that?" Juno asks.

I glare at her for a second because I can't think of a good reason I'm staring at her lips. I tear my eyes away, and unfortunately, they land on the open neckline of her tight uniform polo shirt, where I can see the beginning of the shadowy place, that line that leads to the valley between her breasts.

Pillowy, large breasts. I would never stop touching them if she were mine. My mouth waters.

Like the pebble, I do not know where that thought came from.

I put it out of my head immediately.

"I'm looking at you in no way in particular. Only listening."

She blinks, then wags her head. "If you say so. Anyway. This is my first charter as a chief stew, and I would appreciate it if you could work with me here."

I take a step closer to her. "I am here, and I am working. With you."

She gestures wildly, indicating the entire boat. "I mean, work as a team. Don't make things difficult for me. The guests are difficult enough."

That last part is true. So far, these charters are proving to be far more drama than I bargained for.

"All right, Juno. If the primary wants shitty caviar, I will serve shitty caviar."

Juno clasps her palms together and gives me a slight bow. Adorable but unnecessary.

"Thank you, chef. Hey, I think that is the first time you've ever said my name out loud. I like hearing you say my name," she says, cocking her head.

Juno's lashes are ridiculously long, and they flutter at me when she says those last three words softly.

Another hot pebble drops somewhere deep inside me, and I don't like it.

My gaze drops back down to her cleavage.

"Now. Let's talk dessert, shall we?" She says this casually, unaware that the only dessert I want lies between her legs. Maybe my tongue can stop her tongue from flapping at me all day long.

It's just a fantasy. We are like fire and ice. I'm a man who needs a solitary life, and she's a woman with drive and ambition. She enjoys being a leader, and being a leader requires people to pay attention to you. I cannot afford attention.

Even if we were just two attractive people having fun with each other, it could make her a target. If the Bratva's henchmen were to find me, they would use her, or any other attachments, against me.

Juno may be attractive, but I am trained in self-control. No reason to allow my loneliness to get the better of me now.

Chapter Two

Juno

WHAT EXACTLY IS Maksim's problem with me?

Whatever it is, he'd better get over it quickly. Because we have a lot of meal services to get through over the next week, and if I have to put up with him staring at me like I just grew a second head, I'm going to lose it.

He already gave me enough trouble during the first two charters.

Maksim had muttered curses in Russian every time a dish was returned. I tried to explain that it wasn't personal, and it wasn't my fault.

"Tell them it is cooked perfectly. Explain to them what sous vide is."

I would if I could, but Vanessa was the one who was really good at redirecting the guests. I am good at following the guests' orders, and I'm a mean drink mixer.

On the first few charters of the season, every time I cut

up a twist of lime or reached in the pantry for the olives, Maksim would order me away.

"That is not a proper twist," he would say. "Nothing comes out of my kitchen looking like that."

I tried to remind him that my mixology skills were not a reflection on his galley, but he wasn't hearing me.

This week's charter is a girls' weekend, so maybe we'll get a breather from the drama.

I size up these American influencers as I give them the boat tour.

"Juno, your New Zealand accent is so cute," says the primary, Whitney. I control the urge to roll my eyes.

I'm about to correct her that I'm actually Australian when she asks, "And who is that yummy tattooed Russian man?"

I want to give her my resting bitch face and say, "You mean the chef? Maksim, who you literally were introduced to on the deck five minutes ago?"

But I don't say that. Because I'm a chief stew, who wants a good tip. Scratch that; I'm going to earn us a great tip.

"Oh, that's Maksim. His food is amazing. You won't believe it," I say with the most brilliant smile I can muster.

I cannot believe his skills; that part was true.

From what I've gathered from other crew members, Maksim has no formal training, never went to culinary school, never worked on a boat before. Captain Joe hired him because the man showed up to his interview with his own set of knives and, when asked to show him what he knew, cooked the most perfect steak the captain had ever eaten in his life. The chef had not even been vetted by the yacht staffing agency; Maksim had apparently walked up to the captain and applied. Typical boys' club behavior.

The clincher, however, was Maksim explaining how he

cooked every day for his entire family of 10, from the ripe old age of 12 when his father had run off and his mother sometimes never came home after a bender at her boyfriend's house.

That story made me warm up to Maksim, as much as a person can warm up to him. He keeps everyone at such an arm's length.

"Oh, I love a man who cooks. It's so sexy!" remarks Whitney.

I stifle the urge to disagree. There's nothing inherently more sexy about a man who cooks, no more than a woman who cooks. Even if that man has bedroom eyes and looks like a predator when his eyes drift down to one's cleavage.

I should not be thinking about Maksim's bedroom eyes…those deep pools that glare at me every time I walk through the galley.

"I wouldn't know anything about that," I say.

Bridget, one of the primary's friends, doesn't buy it. "Oh, you're totally into him, I can tell."

God, I hate it when the guests start shipping the crew with each other.

"Me and Maksim? No. No, thank you. I…I think he has a girlfriend or a wife back home in Moscow," I lie.

Why? Why am I trying to throw her off the scent if I don't want her to ship Maksim and me?

The rest of the tour wraps up soon, and I leave the party to confirm lunchtime with Maksim.

Once again, he's gruff with me, though I've done nothing to deserve it.

"Two p.m. lunch?"

I bite my lip as he turns to me in one of his moods. "The preference sheet says 2:30!"

I shrug. "They bumped it up a little. The guests want to swim and then nap before dinner. No big deal."

While the thought about the cabins crosses my mind, I radio Star and the new stew, Juliet, to tell them to stay on top of drink orders. Then, I radio the deck team to ensure the jacuzzi is warming up.

I turn back to Maksim, and he looks like a snorting bull.

"What?" I ask, too loudly. "What now?" We're less than an hour into this trip, and I'm already done with him.

"We were in the middle of a conversation, and you started talking to the crew like I wasn't even here," he says.

Is he for real? "I'm sorry, I thought we were done with this conversation."

A strange smile stretches his lips, half sneer and half lethal. "We end conversations when I say we end them. You do not get to make decisions about mealtimes."

Oh, really? If he thinks his low, quiet, predatory voice will do something to me, he's quite wrong. "A guest is entitled to change her mind. They pay a lot of fucking money to make last-minute changes. Remember the impromptu royal birthday beach party?"

Through gritted teeth, he snarls, "The food is not going to be ready at two. Stall them. That's your job."

Huffing, I tell him, "Maybe you should go speak with the primary. Whitney's already got the hots for you; she'd probably do anything you say."

Is it me, or did he take a step closer?

His fists ball. "I don't want to talk to the primary. I don't have any interest in the whims of spoiled women who have never been told no. You," he says, this time clearly stepping closer to me, "finesse them."

My breath catches. An evergreen and cedar scent hits my nostrils. Why is he so close that I can smell his body wash? And why do I like it?

I do not appreciate how he said that word, "finesse." It

was too deep, too low. Too gravelly. It scrapes across me like fangs on skin, looking for the most sensitive, juiciest place to bite.

I grit my teeth right back at him. "No."

His nostrils flare, and somehow, this flips a switch inside me. His heated gaze dances across my skin. Maksim speaks a single word. I don't know what it is, but the sound of it feels like melting ice cream on a hot day. "Pchelka."

I square my shoulders and suck in my breath. I don't care how good he smells; he does not speak to me that way. "I don't know what you just said, but you can kiss my psh…pshulka, and have that food ready to serve at two. Make a charcuterie board. You'll figure it out. You're the genius chef, after all."

I sashay from the galley, pretending I have some urgent business elsewhere.

I can still hear him muttering outside on the sky deck as I begin setting the table for lunch.

Maybe that stern daddy energy works on Moscow girls, but it isn't going to get him anywhere with Juno from Melbourne.

I've got too much to prove to let this man distract me with his mysterious nicknames and beautiful eyebrows.

Chapter Three

Maksim

THAT WOMAN. That woman is going to be the death of me.

Calm down, Maksim, and focus. What do you have ready to appease the guests while they wait for the main lunch course?

I pull together a platter of fruit and nuts. When I finish, the new second stew, Juliet, comes into the galley, and I have her bring the tray up.

When my back is turned to the door while I'm sautéing the chicken to go with the salad lunch they've ordered for the main course, I can feel a thunderous presence entering the galley. I know her before she speaks.

"Chef?"

"That's me." I don't turn around.

"You were supposed to send up a charcuterie. What's with the fruit and shit?"

My blood is not boiling, because I will not let it.

"Are they happy?"

"They're hungry," Juno says, emphasizing the last word as if I don't know that my entire job is to address everyone's hunger on this boat.

The chicken is now done; I plate it with the Caesar salads, not making eye contact with Juno.

"Lunch is ready now," I say.

"They have been asking for lunch for twenty minutes. You didn't give me much to work with."

When the last plate is ready, I chuck my serving spoon into the sink with a clatter, then turn to face Juno. "And if I sent up meat and cheese, they would not be hungry for salad, and half of this would go to waste!"

Juno's eyes widen. "Why are you yelling? It's not even dinner service, and already you're impossible!" she seethes.

"Why are you so wasteful with food?!"

Fire flashes in her eyes, and there's something else there. I could be wrong, but her bottom lip trembles, just a hair. No, I'm not mistaken. I did see it. Something I said hit a nerve.

With a resolute look, she radios the girls to come to the galley to bring up the plates. In the second before Juliet and Star whisk into the room, she quietly delivers her reply to me, jabbing the air with her radio for emphasis.

"Fuck. You."

Then, she loads up her arms with the dishes and disappears, leaving me chilled to the bone, my blood coursing wildly.

Chapter Four

Juno

My mind is distracted during the meeting with my other stews later that afternoon.

There's a lot of pressure on me for this first dinner service. Vanessa, my former chief stew was exceptionally talented with tablescapes and theme parties. These guests want a Wild West theme tonight, and I'm at a loss.

"I've done plenty of Gatsby parties, disco themes, casino nights. But never a Wild West theme," says Juliet, my second stew. Her experience on boats is why I made her my second rather than Star when Vanessa left after finding out she was pregnant.

"Me neither," I say, looking at the meager on-theme decorations sent over by the provisioner. I wish I'd looked more closely when we'd unloaded the truck, but I was too focused on the food and other essentials. Some straw cowboy hats, a few red bandanas, a red checked picnic blanket. I sigh and think. "This stuff looks like a kid's birthday party."

Star pipes up with, "Can we get an upright piano? You know, to make the room look like a saloon?"

She looks so earnest, I don't have the heart to say what I want to say. Where would we get an upright piano last minute, in the middle of the sea? Even if someone in Naples had one, how would it get here? By tender? It would sink the vessel like a stone.

"If only," I say, resisting the urge to pat Star on her pretty little head.

Then it hits me. "Wait! I have a thought," I say.

"What, what is it?" Juliet asks.

Since my last confrontation with the chef, the word "finesse" has stuck in my brain. He might be a bit of an ogre, but the suggestion has worked its way into me. When my younger twin sisters celebrated their tenth birthday, they'd wanted a dragon theme. We'd had no money for decorations. But we did have some second-hand dinosaur toys, piles of donated clothes that didn't fit, costume jewelry, and construction paper. With scissors, tape, and hot glue, I had used what we had and turned dinosaurs into dragons, and my sisters woke up to a whole house that had been transformed into an underground lair.

"Girls, go pull everything you can find out of the closets. Linens, party supplies, all of it. We're gonna cannibalize this bitch."

Star gasps.

"Oh, honey. We're not actually going to eat a human. It's an expression."

The poor girl sighs, and her sweet face looks so much like my younger sister that I can't help but grasp her hand and smile at her relief.

Vanessa might have been a genius with finessing the

guests, legendary with her table decorations. But my exceptional talent, even outside of yachting, is resourcefulness and tenacity.

With the girls off to gather supplies, I take a moment to gather up my courage to talk to the chef about dinner.

"Don't be scared, Juno. He's just another chef with a huge ego. You got this."

I grab my radio; I'm ready for this. Thank god I don't have to have every conversation in person.

As soon as I turn around to begin ransacking some of the salon storage, I run smack dab into a wall. I bounce back and look up. It's not a wall but a barrel chest.

"Oh!" I exclaim, stumbling.

"I didn't mean to scare you," the brick wall says, steadying me with a thick forearm.

Inside, I cringe as my eyes travel upward to face a startled Maksim. He heard what I'd just said.

His deep, dark eyes scan my face, and I prepare to be dressed down about the ego comment. Maksim's expression is unreadable, though. It's part of what makes him so difficult to deal with. I never know if he's happy, sad, angry, or something else. Scratch that; I definitely know when he's angry. He's fucking grumpy as hell all the time.

"I just came to find you to confirm the timeline for the dinner courses tonight."

His voice is even, if slightly lower and softer than usual.

I match his tone. "You could have just radioed me."

Ever so slightly, his top lip pulls up. Is that...a smile? Maybe under a microscope, it might pass for a smile. "But then, I would miss the chance to hear about my giant ego."

Is he hurt? Upset? Indifferent? I can't tell. I almost wish he'd get angry or offended because I know how to deal with his thunder. I do not know how to deal with him when he's quiet and...flirty? Is that what he's doing right now?

He's standing close to me, neither of us having bothered to back away since that collision with my boobs to his brick-wall chest.

"I think you're intimately familiar with your own ego," I say, inwardly cursing at how raspy my voice sounds.

That full, hard lip twitches, but barely. I've been staring at that lip for a second too long. Quickly meeting Maksim's gaze again, I see something in his eyes that makes my insides turn to jelly.

"I am; I would like to hear you say the words. How giant is it?"

I swallow. "So big, it has its own separate circulatory system. Where your soul should be." I don't know if that makes any sense, but I don't really care. Words are just falling out. Surely, though, he can take it.

"That's big. Tell me more," he says.

"Why, so you can stroke it?"

He lifts one shoulder, and that devilish lip twitches again. "I'm pretty good at pumping myself up. But I'd rather you do it."

Those last six words land somewhere below my navel and vibrate there for a second. Are we still talking about his ego?

I force my face into a flat expression. I'm not giving him what he wants. "You wish."

Those thick, brown eyebrows rise, turning his forehead into deep furrows. I don't know if that look is surprised or amused. I hate that I can't read him. It's so aggravating. He's the most infuriating person I've ever met.

It seems like we're playing a game of chicken, both of us daring the other to look away. His stare is lethal, turning my jellied insides to liquid. Something tells me he doesn't lose this game, ever. There's an unsettling fearlessness behind those eyes. The kind of eyes that have seen some shit. But he hasn't tried a staring contest with me. I've seen some shit, too. Maksim is the first person who could possibly intimidate me if he really wanted to.

To my shock, he looks away then clears his throat. "Why don't we sit down and go over tonight's courses."

And just like that, the moment is over. Whatever that moment was. One second he seems like he can't take his eyes off my mouth, and the next minute, he's super professional.

Together, we make the plan for dinner. Maksim lists the courses he'll be serving: caviar appetizers, lobster bisque, dandelion greens salad, and a main course of duck barbecue and cornbread, as a nod to the Wild West theme. With a fig-orange reduction, of course, because we have to keep it five-star. Dessert will be his take on a wild berry crumble, which incorporates some sort of magical flavored foam to elevate it. I have never eaten foam and never want to eat it, but I trust it will be good. Not a lot of this dinner is overtly Wild West, but at this point, I don't have the energy to push back. It's all going to be delicious, and the guests will be thrilled. My mouth waters at the words, the descriptions, and the way he says them. It's not just the accent, but he's extra patient with me, so I know how to describe the food to the guests. I, in turn, walk him through how the other stews, and I plan on coordinating the timing, so everything flows smoothly. There's an art to serving, like dance choreography. It can be lovely to witness when it's all executed well. Even if we're all dressed up like old-timey dancing girls and cowboys, the attention to detail goes a long way.

Throughout this shockingly civil conversation, my mind is reeling. How can a man flip a switch so quickly? How does he shift from heated banter to professional? We

hadn't had time to explore whatever was passing
between us.

And what was it? And, do I want to explore it? Maybe
someday, with somebody, but him? No. Not Maksim. He's
too cold, too closed off. Too surly and too…I don't know.
Loaded down with baggage. Probably. Just a guess.

Baggage is one thing I do not need. I've only gotten
free of my own. A mismatched, heavy set of suitcases
containing uplifting stories such as childhood hunger, alcoholic father, crippling debt. All of that has been sorted. My
siblings are fine, my father is in treatment, and thanks to
my hustling, there's a house I own free and clear back in
Melbourne. I'm good. I don't need a man. If I did, I don't
need one in my life that needs fixing. I've finished fixing
myself and my family. I'm done with that.

When we wrap up the meeting, the yacht lurches in the
waves right at the moment when I stand. I know how to stay
upright in moments like this, yet the turbulence catches me
off guard. I stumble, reaching out to steady myself against
the dining room table. But before my hand touches wood,
something else has me. Two bulky forearms grab mine, rough
fingers gripping me and pulling me close to that brick wall.

"I'm fine," I say.

"Hold on, here comes another one," he says, too close
to my ear. In fact, everything about Maksim is too near.
But I don't have time to think about the shivers running
down my spine because the boat crests another wave and
slams down hard on the other side.

"Jesus," I breathe, preparing for us to fall.

It's then that I notice that Maksim is not holding on to
anything. How? How does this man who has never worked
on a boat before have sea legs this adept? I can't resist the
urge to look down. Maybe those massive thighs have some-

thing to do with that. His feet planted wide, he has me clamped against him until the waters steady.

"The sea is choppy today," he says.

"Hopefully, the captain will find a calm spot soon. Don't want our guests chucking up chicken Caesar. What a waste."

Our eyes connect, both of us smirking as we remember the conversation from before, when he'd told me his opinion of my wastefulness.

"Chucking up?" he repeats, and for the first time, he looks amused.

I don't know how long we stand here like this. After some time, it occurs to me that we are through the waves now, yet the chef's hands are still on me. His chest is still pressing against my mine with every breath. His warmth radiates through that unnecessarily tight tee-shirt.

Does he realize it, too?

Now seems like a good time to ruin this nice-ish moment. "I wonder if you could do the girls and me a favor tonight."

"No," he says, his body stiffening, an eyebrow arching.

"You don't even know what it is yet."

"Every time a chief stew says that to someone, it always ends up with crewmates dressed ridiculously, performing like show horses for the guests. No, thank you."

I huff. "You make a lot of assumptions, especially for someone who keeps to himself all the time."

"And why do you think that is?" he asks, still not letting go of me. Why am I not pushing him away?

"Because you're super fun at parties," I reply, cocking my head.

"No, I am not. I've never heard such a wild accusation," he retorts. "In fact, I keep to myself because poor Dustin had to put on a grass skirt and a coconut bra on the first charter. I heard Elijah talking about everyone performing a rap battle on another boat he worked on. Ridiculous. I will not be joining in."

I've never been one to use my feminine wiles to get my way. That's not my style. And still, I can't help but feel this thing between us. Maybe it has something to do with the tree branch below his waist pressing against my thigh. Good lord.

I lean back and tilt my head slightly to the side, daring to close the distance between us. My lips are so close to his I can feel his breath. His jaw ticks. When our eyes meet, I flutter my lashes and ask, oh so sweetly, "Please? Just one. Tiny. Little. Favor?"

A low growl from deep inside his chest vibrates against my breasts. I lean away a bit more, trying to crack the code of his face.

He doesn't allow that. Instead, Maksim abruptly tightens his hold on me, his arms like a vise. Through clenched teeth, he rasps, "What are you doing, little girl? Don't fuck with me. Don't you dare."

This time, I end the moment first.

"Fine," I chirp brightly, shrugging. "I don't need your help. The rest of the crew, the team players, can handle the entertainment. I'm sure cowboy movies are another stupid thing to you. No big deal."

His beautiful eyebrows come together, and he opens his mouth to speak.

Just then, the captain strolls into the salon.

"Sorry about the turbulence back there. I just came to see if anything broke in here. Oh. Sorry to interrupt."

Maksim lets me go roughly, and I snap away. Why do I feel like we've been caught doing something wrong?

"You were not interrupting anything," Maksim says, too loudly. He sounds stilted and not like himself.

I don't make us look any less guilty of canoodling on the job when I add, "Nope! Nothing! I was choking, and he was helping me."

The captain looks at me and then at Maksim. "I don't know how you kids made it through your maritime first aid course, but here's a tip. Next time something like that happens, you gotta take her from behind, big guy. Real firm, like this. I mean, really give it to her."

Maksim quietly puffs air out of his nose. Was that a laugh?

Captain Joe mimes the Heimlich maneuver while I fight off the urge to throw myself overboard.

Why is this my life?

Chapter Five

Maksim

I CANNOT BELIEVE I'm doing this, I think, as I look at myself in the mirror. Dinner service finished, I fished out costume pieces from the box that Juliet brought to the galley for the crew to adorn themselves with. Before thinking better of it, I grabbed several pieces.

I look ridiculous. My chef's jacket has been replaced by a button-up shirt with fringe all down the sleeve, made of cut-up linen napkins. On my chest is a sheriff star fashioned from old kitchen utensils. And on my head, the dumbest-looking straw cowboy hat that ever existed. I look like an entertainer at a child's party. A sad, sad entertainer.

What has happened to me?

Well, I'm not doing this for Juno. That's for sure. I'm doing this because this whole plan is an affront to cowboy movies, and I have to salvage what I can.

Juno was wrong. I'm a bit of a cowboy movie

aficionado. I absolutely love John Wayne. Clint Eastwood. All of them. Rooster Cogburn is my idol.

Plus, I'm in a good mood. Well, not good. A service-able mood. Dinner went off far more smoothly than usual. I chalk that up to Juno and I keeping our opinions to ourselves. Not once did I provoke her to argue with me over something petty. Likewise, she was strangely quiet.

So quiet that people noticed.

"What is going on with you two?" Elijah had asked after Juno had left the galley to deliver dessert earlier.

Without thinking, I had blurted, "We're not doing anything wrong."

The Bahamian bosun had just stared and blinked at me for a second, rubbed the brown skin of his chin, then shook his head and went on with helping serve the dessert course. Shortly after that, I'd heard Andre, the new deck-hand from Brazil, cackling to himself while washing up dishes.

I almost said something, but I kept it to myself.

"Are you ready?" Star asks, peeking into my bathroom via the door I'd left ajar. She's wearing sparkly feathers in her hair, purloined from the Mardi Gras decorations, and shimmery tablecloth cinched around her waist. It looks more like a toga than a dancing girl from the 1800s, but I say nothing. The guests will be too drunk to notice.

I nod curtly and follow her and Juliet to the sky deck.

The other deckhand, a young Canadian named Dustin, snickers as we pass through the galley.

"You have something you'd like to say to me, friend?" I puff my chest out, ready to remind him how equally ridiculous he looks in his impromptu cowboy uniform.

Juno looks at me in this getup and covers her mouth in shock.

She passes out the script from my favorite John Wayne

movie. Apparently, we are to reenact a scene, and my gut tumbles in anxiety. I soldier on, determined not to let these heathens ruin the good name of John Wayne.

The scene lasts all of five minutes and ends with raucous, drunken applause from the guests.

I nod my head in gratitude and quickly disappear into the galley. Juno stands in my way.

"Excuse me," I say.

She shakes her head. "Not so fast. The guests want to meet you." The glint in her eye is full of amusement. She is enjoying every second of my humiliation, her arms crossed in satisfaction.

Releasing a quiet sigh, I reluctantly turn and politely nod my head at the guests' table.

"He's out of uniform, but Mr. John Wayne is your chef."

More applause. More cheers. More humiliation. I grit my teeth and smile, reminding myself this is all for the tip.

Juno is clapping too, but not smiling. Something else is there in her eyes, and I can't figure out what she's thinking. Perhaps I overacted or didn't do enough. Maybe she will follow me into the galley to chew me out over one thing or another. It wouldn't be the first time. But still, I find my face softening when we look at each other across the room.

I nod again, summoning all of my ability to accept compliments, which is not much. Suddenly I'm overcome with a strange feeling that I have to get out of here. Never have I had this many pairs of eyes on me. Never. I am a man who operates behind the scenes. I am a man who hides in the shadows, strikes, disappears, and collects a paycheck. I am the reaper. I was the reaper. I had thought working as a chef would allow me to stay behind the scenes, but now I'm in the spotlight, dressed like a buffoon.

I must get out of here immediately.

I stalk through the galley, brushing past Juno. I don't care if I seem rude; I've done enough. I am not a show pony. Bits and pieces of the cowboy costume are left on the floor as I rip and tear, making my way down the stairs, through the crew mess, and down the hall toward my cabin.

Finally, I am rid of every last bit of the costume when a hand touches my shoulder from behind. The sound of my pulse races in my ears.

"Maksim."

Whirling around, I meet Juno's gaze. "There was a time, little girl, when someone sneaking up behind me would end up…." I stop myself. What am I saying? She doesn't know about my past. And she can't know. It's profoundly upsetting stuff.

"I…I just wanted to say thank you," she says softly.

Clinging to my cold demeanor, I reply, "I did it for the tips. Like you said."

The brightness dims in her shining eyes. "Oh," she says, nodding, her voice higher than usual. "Well. Thank you for that. Either way, it was nice."

She turns to leave, and something drops in my stomach. A hot stone lands deep in my gut; this time, the ripples send out waves of emotion that cause me to act before I think. I reach out and grab her upper arm as she turns away.

"Juno," I say. "Wait."

"What?" Juno asks, her face slightly pained, annoyed. This woman shows the world exactly how she feels all of the time, and the only feeling I give her is heartburn. I am a roiling sea beneath the surface, and I share it with no one.

"I…"

"Yes?"

Cursing, I let it out. "Fuck. I did it for you."

Juno's lips spread in a catlike grin. She cocks her head. "I know." Those soft shimmery lips set in a satisfied smile make my cock twitch to life. Not to mention how that dancing girl costume she's fashioned out of table linens is falling open, exposing her breasts that have been trussed up in some kind of insanely frilly push-up bra. The black lace edges her supple skin, and my mouth salivates.

The self-satisfied look on her face will drive me insane with the need to fix her attitude completely. I'm tired from cooking all day, but I could muster enough energy if necessary.

I could give those pouty lips something better to do. How would they feel, wrapped around my cock? Moaning on it. Sucking. Fucking swallowing all of me.

It takes all of my strength to say good night.

But my better self, my logical self, takes hold. I can't do this.

I can't let myself get attached.

I nod and turn away. The galley can be cleaned in the morning. I'll wake up early. God knows I won't sleep tonight.

Chapter Six

Juno

No FUCKING WAY is he walking away from me like that. I follow him down here, and that's all he has to say?

"Maksim, wait."

I couldn't sound more like a scared, desperate little girl if I tried. My hand on his arm is all it takes, though.

The chef rounds on me. He brushes my hand from his arm only to grab my face in both his rough hands in one swift motion.

"What, Juno? What. The fuck. Do you want?"

My breath like fire in my lungs, I answer, "I want to know what changed your mind."

His jaw clenches. "To get you to leave me alone. So I wouldn't have to hear the words 'team player' ever leave your mouth again."

I spit out the words, "Fuck you. That's not why."

His eyes are wild, his teeth are bared. I cannot wait to hear what he says next.

He says nothing. Amid that charged silence, Maksim kisses me.

The contact makes the world around us dim while my insides explode. His full, hard lips press against mine with a fire that turns my liquid nerves into molten lava. I don't know what to do with my hands; it's been so long since someone has grabbed me and kissed me like this. So I rest them against his chest, tentatively. At this gentle touch, he deepens the kiss, his tongue licking the seam of my mouth. I open to him, and our tongues slide past each other. Maksim's lips and tongue take over the whole of my senses. He tastes like wild berries and salted caramel. Internally, I smile. I'd been craving a sample of that dessert all evening. This is better. Far, far better.

The world around us changes to a hazy, rosy pink when the chef's rough thumb rubs slowly up and down my cheek.

I'm kissing Maksim. Maksim is kissing me. How did I get here? I know how. The moment he'd shown up dressed in that half-assed costume I'd made and then said those lines and didn't hold back an ounce? I never could have predicted that. I thought about how hard he would have had to work to set aside his ego, that cool darkness he carries around like an emblem. And the thought of that pushed aside everything else. I knew he'd done it for me. He'd done it to help me leave an impression on the guests, help me succeed.

This man takes everything with his kisses. His tongue lingers, leaving nothing untouched, unexplored. He angles his face more, then moves his hands back, tangling his fingers in my hair. My curls are being held in place with bobby pins and clips, with silly pipe curls hanging around my face. When his fingers contact the pins, he growls into my mouth. I gasp as I feel tugging, then loosening. Then, a plink of metal hits the wood floor. More tugging, more loosening. Another plink. Maksim is removing each of my hairpins, never stopping to look at what he's doing. No, he's far too busy making me lose my breath and lose every last bit of sound judgment with his juicy mouth.

All the hairpins are gone; Maksim thrusts his thick fingers through my hair, cupping my scalp. I'm going to be a tangled mess. My makeup will advertise to everyone what I've been doing down here. But no one else is around. Everyone else is upstairs, helping clean up or serving drinks, hoping the guests will give up and go to bed soon.

Bed. Is that where this is going? The way he kisses seems to indicate that yes, that's where this is headed.

And the way his fingertips roughly massage my scalp, like he can't get enough of touching my hair. Everything feels so good; I lose myself in the moment and moan into his mouth.

He pulls away. Still close, but seemingly waking up from a dream. With his brow furrowed again, he looks so severe. Breathless, determined, and yet holding back. His nostrils flare. His forearm ripples as he continues to grip my face, my hair.

"What are you fighting in there?" I ask, tracing a fingertip across his wrinkled forehead.

"Nothing," he answers. "I am thinking."

I smile, my gaze falling to those lovely, firm lips. "Tell me what you're thinking; maybe I can help."

"If I told you, we'd end up fighting again."

I shouldn't ask. "Why?"

"Because I would say it all wrong."

I shake my head, then let my hands drift lower until my palm lands again on his sternum. "Then don't think. Stop thinking and just let me in. Tell me what you want."

He curses, then grits out the words. "You. In my bed. Now."

Throwing all caution to the wind, I nod my head yes. "Let's go."

The second his door clicks shut, his mouth is on me again. But this time, the real Maksim has been freed. His kiss out in the hallway was a small letting go of something. This time, he is letting loose. Both of us are.

Someone or something has broken a spell. His mouth claims me, his tongue surging into my mouth with energy that threatens to blot out the memory of all previous kisses.

I didn't think it was possible to kiss this intensely, but still, he wants more. His body needs more; I can feel it. And so does mine.

I've never been so utterly lost in another person's touch before. No one has ever felt this passionate. Certainly not someone who this morning was driving me insane with his lousy attitude.

The friction of our bodies sparks heat through my clothes, and my nipples harden against his torso. More. I need more. I scramble against him, generating more heat, more friction, more of everything.

I don't want to make love to him, and I don't want him to make love to me. I want him to screw me. Fuck me. Pin me to the wall, or the bed, or, hell, the floor. I don't give a fuck.

I'm so tired of his attitude; I'm going to fuck that surly look off his stupid, beautiful face.

The next thing I know, Maksim's hands are full of this tablecloth I'm wearing as a dress.

He rumbles. "I'm going to take this ridiculous costume off you now."

"Do it," I rasp. "Wreck it if you're man enough."

Fabric tape tears. Seams shred. Pins fly. And Maksim is

left holding bits of my costume in his two fists. I'm left in nothing but my frilly underwear and bra.

His chest heaves as he growls, gesturing at my tits with a lift of his chin. "Why in god's name do you have that with you on the boat?"

I cluck. "I saw it in a little store in Monaco, and I thought it was cute. I thought I might have a chance to wear it for somebody."

His eyes widen, his throat bobs. The chef lowers his chin and looks up at me with the gaze of a truly pissed-off animal in a cage. He croaks, "Who is the fucking somebody?"

I should tell him he's misinterpreted what I've said. There is nobody, in particular, I had in mind when I bought this thing. And I cannot stress enough that under normal everyday circumstances, I do not care at all for a man who thinks he can claim a woman for himself. Or for a man who gets jealous when there is no relationship, to begin with.

But Maksim. The way he seethes. The way I enjoy poking this bear. I want to explore this further.

"I asked, who is the fucking guy?" he repeats.

I let the shy smile continue the narrative rather than allowing my words to tell an outright lie. I break eye contact and look down at the floor, at my aching feet. You'd think working in bare feet to keep the teak floor clean would be fun, but it is actually murder on one's joints. The ache in my soles is nothing compared to the throbbing inside my soaked panties. Can he see? Can he tell? He must know how maddeningly turned on he made me with that kiss. Anyone would be utterly thirsty for a good lay after a kiss like that. Feeling self-conscious about the wetness spreading over my panties, I cross one foot over the other.

By me not answering him, his breathing grows harder. He doesn't touch me, but Maksim is right in my face in the next second. "Who?"

If I weren't so observant and so bloody horny, I might be scared of him like this. But I've seen the kindness in his eyes. Yes, I've seen the dark Maksim. The haunted Maksim. But now, I see nothing but the mad craving, and it matches mine.

All I say is, "You wouldn't understand." And he's all over me like warm butter on toast.

The chef half growls, half groans into my mouth as his hands tug and shove at the lace. My breasts spill out over cups of my bra. He groans again but pulls away from the kiss to study them. I gasp at the contact of his palms and roughened fingers over the tender skin, over my hardened nipples.

"Who?" he asks again, but the word is slightly fainter, his gaze locked on my tits. Can't blame the poor guy, actually. They are pretty great tits.

What else is great? Chef's hands. Scarred from years of burns and cuts and god knows what else he's done to himself in kitchens, the scrape of those fingers is sending me into orbit. The lava in my belly sends arcs of heat to every limb, every finger and toe. I desperately want to touch him, but he's enjoying this too much. I'm reveling in the white-hot jealousy over someone who doesn't even exist.

"Tell me, pchelka."

"No," I whisper.

His jaw tightens, and his thumb and forefinger roll my left nipple. I nearly buckle from the explosion of sensation.

And then, he angles his head downward, sucking the opposite nipple into his brazen mouth. I inhale sharply, whimpering as his teeth scrape that tight peak.

He pops my nipple from his mouth. "Tell me before I rip that bra to shreds, as I did to the costume."

That mouth then resumes kissing me tenderly, almost reverently, over every sensitive inch of my breasts. He hums, murmurs words I don't understand, whispers sweet nothings, and rubs his chin's scruff against them. Inside, I am a mess.

My voice trembles despite my efforts to seem resolute. "This is a hand-stitched designer push-up bra. Don't you fucking dare."

His voice—fuck him for sounding so outrageously sexy —drops an octave and reverberates somewhere dark, empty, and needy. "Pchelka, I will buy you three of them in any color you want."

I huff out a laugh. "You'll hurt me."

"You won't feel a thing, Juno."

"Bullshit."

The chef pauses, lifts his head, and meets my gaze. My body stills. No way. No way he's going to do it. He clamps one hand over the edge. In the next breath, with his eyes trained on mine, the sound of ripping material fills the corridor.

He was right. It didn't hurt. Why didn't it hurt?

I look down between my legs, and my bra is torn in two on the floor.

He thinks he's won.

I look back up into his eyes. "I lied. I wear sexy things for myself. Just me, and nobody else."

Something about this fact lights a fire under this man because the next thing I know, I am under him.

We are on his bed, with me in nothing but my lace panties, and Maksim is on top of me, planted between my legs and destroying every inch of me with his mouth. He will wreck me, and I welcome it with my fire.

This is what happens when I push him too far. And I'm proud of myself. Because this solid brick house of a beast is filling in all the cracks. Maybe not in my heart, but down in the long-neglected valleys of my sex. Human touch is so undervalued until you're on a boat for weeks at a time.

Is that what this is? Desperation for human touch? A boatmance? Maybe that's fine. Being constantly on opposite ends of arguments has driven us to this.

My lips will be so swollen from kissing they might be bruised. I'm going to end up with love bites all over my chest and tits. And now, this wild man has lain waste to my panties and is knocking my thighs apart with his shoulders.

Holy shit. It's happening.

I look down between my legs, and the sight makes me nearly lose consciousness. His forehead is furrowed in concentration. And those lips, tongue, and teeth? Are absolutely destroying my pussy.

Combined with the wet, suctioning noises, the sensations make my eyes roll back in my head.

Was this what I had in mind when I'd thought about fucking him into a better attitude? Because it seems like what's happening here is he's fucking the words out of my mouth. Fucking me with so much vigorous attention I might pass out.

I'll never be able to simply look him in the eye again after this and discuss dinner service. Not without remembering this tongue lashing me more thoroughly than his ornery words could ever do.

Chapter Seven

Maksim

JUNO TASTES like the woodland honey from my childhood. It's like heaven, the kind of heaven you experience when you're too young to realize the sweetness comes to an end.

Now I am an adult, hurtling my way to hell. And yet, with Juno underneath me, in my bed, it's like I've been given a second taste of heaven on my tongue.

I can't get enough of her. Her sweet essence fills me, coats my lips, drips down my chin. I am utterly lost.

I barely recall how we got here. Another silly argument, another pointless disagreement, and we'd found we had no words left, only urges. Mine are the urges of a simple animal: to tear at clothes, drag her to my cave and claim her body.

Any thoughts about the risk of attachment have gone out the porthole. If Bratva comes for me, so be it.

I'd had a mind to fuck the attitude out of her, fix her, make her behave. But now, it seems like I am hopeless.

She's too sweet and too spicy all at once. She is not a woman to be tamed. She is not a woman for me to own or control.

She is a woman who will wreck herself and me in the process.

But I will not stop. I don't have to stop tonight.

My teeth and lips find her taut clit. My lips circle it, sucking it gently into my mouth, and Juno's thighs begin to tremble. Her back arches off the bed; she's so close to coming.

I breathe against her damp folds. "Don't come yet, kisa."

My kitten bucks against my face, and I pull back.

"No, no, little girl. What did I say?"

"Fuck you."

"Naughty," I murmur, placing a soft kiss on the inside of her thigh.

I am a big talker, but in truth, I am tormented by her soft moans, her dripping cunt, her whimpering. But this is where my talent lies. Torture and death are my expertise on land. On this boat, I'm going to torture this saucy woman with my tongue.

I adjust her so that her thighs rest on my shoulders. Her gasp at my brute strength strokes my ego; I'm not going to pretend it doesn't.

I sweep my tongue over her folds, slipping it into her tightness, every tiny noise from her pushing me closer to the edge. I savor being so close to losing control, but will myself to hold on. I'm not finished with her. Once more, I clamp my mouth around her clit, and, one hand letting go of its grip against her outer thigh, I sink one finger inside her heat. Then another. The slow stroking inside her sweet wetness churns up my desire. My need for her threatens to blot out all reason.

Juno, my pchelka, my ever-buzzing little bee, can hold out no longer. Her release breaks over her in waves, and she squeaks out my name.

"Maksim," she says softly. Too softly. "Maksim. Oh my god."

My mouth isn't finished with her. I'm not done feasting on her, drinking in her sweet honey, covering myself with her scent.

We're all far too trained to keep quiet on this boat. As I kiss my way back up her soft belly, sharing her taste with her, I accidentally allow my mind to wander.

"As soon as we have more privacy, I want to hear you shout my name, zaya, my little bunny."

I roll onto my back with Juno flopped onto my chest, limp from her release. She lifts her head. "What did you say?"

I said something I should not have said. I cannot promise her more rendezvous such as this one.

"I should not be so presumptuous to assume you'd want to do that again," I say.

She laughs. "Calm down. I'm not going to ask you to marry me. We can't stand each other, remember? That was all of five minutes ago."

I pop up, hitting my head on the bunk above us, and curse. "Five minutes, my ass."

"You are too much," she says. "And far too easy to tease."

I exhale, closing my eyes and enjoying the play of her soft fingers through the fuzz of my chest.

I grumble, "I am not easy to tease. You are simply relentless in your teasing."

She rolls over until she's nearly on top of me. "Relentless? Some have called me fiery. Ambitious. Headstrong. But relentless and a tease? Maybe only with you."

A chuckle escapes me. "With me, you are the definition of teasing the cock."

"I am not a cock tease!"

"Fine," I breathe. "You're not a cock tease."

I say no more but glance down at the pole tenting the blanket at my pelvis.

She follows my gaze, then looks back up in my eyes. Those deep green irises torture me with the mischief that constantly whirls through her wicked brain.

A tongue darts out, wet and pink, to lick her lips as one finger plays with one of my nipples.

Juno's voice is low and husky. "I'm not a tease. Because teases don't do this."

With those words, Juno disappears under the blanket.

Heat explodes through me when her soft lips press a kiss to the tip.

"Juno," I groan. "Fuck."

She hums on it, taking the tip into her mouth. My blood has left my brain entirely. Every nerve ending is on fire. She takes in more, swirling and licking, sucking and devouring. My mind flips back to when I saw her deep throating an ice cream cone on our last night out with the crew. She'd been drunk, so I'd had to keep a close eye on her. I didn't trust some of the other crew members.

She'd made a mess of herself, vanilla ice cream dripping down her chest. And I wonder why I couldn't sleep that night until I had given myself some relief.

But this, this is by far better than what came to mind whenever I thought of the ice cream incident. She takes more of it until I'm buried inside her, and her head begins to bob.

Cursing in pleasure, I tear the blanket away to watch her go to town on me.

This girl is going to be the end of me. I've never seen

anyone so committed, so in the moment. She's actually enjoying it.

I reach down and thread my fingers through her hair. Brushing it away from her face, I catch her looking up at me. I hold my breath, and my body tightens. Our eyes locked together, I can feel my cock hitting the back of her throat. Her eyes leak tears.

"My pchelka, you can stop if you—oh fucking fuck…." My words get lost as my balls tighten. At the exact moment, Juno opens her throat and takes me down, all of me, and I explode.

My cum races down her throat, and she swallows.

Mine. She's mine.

I nearly black out from the momentary pleasure of it.

The tightness that has had a hold on my body suddenly relaxes.

"Juno," I mumble.

My eyes closed, I let the pleasure radiate through me. This time, when another hot pebble drops inside my stomach, the rippling effect is nothing but warmth, light, and…home.

Not home in the woods of Siberia. Not home in my cold, spartan apartment in Moscow. But home is something as simple as belonging. Connecting.

Bonding.

"But please, tell me more about how I'm a tease."

My eyes fly open to see Juno, her lips arced in a satisfied smile.

I say nothing but reach up to cup her face. I hold her like that for a moment until the smile on her face transforms into something else.

. . .

"I DIDN'T JUST PUT on the stupid cowboy costume to help you succeed, Juno."

She looks confused. "Then, what was the other reason?"

I run the tip of my finger over her lip.

"Too much of what I do pisses you off. For once, I wanted to do something to make you smile."

Chapter Eight

Juno

"What are you so smiley about?"

Startled, I look up from my breakfast prep to see Elijah washing down the deck and giving me a weird look.

"What do you mean? When am I not smiling? Am I not a smiling person?"

I babble on and on because I know what he saw. He saw me grinning ear to ear while setting out dishes and forks and flowers for the table. A specific, dopey grin that a person only has when they just got laid.

"You look like you got up to no good last night," he says with a wink.

Both of us department heads, we are equal in rank. And, since Vanessa left, the closest person I would consider a friend on this vessel.

"I wouldn't say no good. I would say very, very good." The laughter that comes from me is girlish, not like me at all.

"Who is it? Spill it," Elijah asks, not pausing as he sprays down the teak.

"The only other person on this boat I don't outrank other than you," I say, a hand on my hip.

His eyes widen in mock horror. "The captain!?"

I snort and chuck an orange at him, which he dodges while laughing.

"Since you're going to make me say it. Maksim and I sorta hooked up last night."

Elijah laughs and says, "Yeah, we were all wondering when you would give in to the crackling sexual tension."

I bristle at this. Only a little because I know he means well. That's how things go on these boats. People hook up, and then they get over it. The crew ships couples all the time, but nobody ever takes it seriously.

"Can we expect fewer fireworks in the galley then?" he asks, his eyes still laughing.

Blowing out a sigh, I say, "You know what? I…I kind of have real feelings for the guy. The whole cowboy thing last night…he said he wouldn't do it, and I didn't push. But then he did because he just wanted to see me smile."

I finish my work at the table and look up at Elijah, waiting for him to tell me to be careful. We don't know much about Maksim, so I should guard my feelings until I know him better.

"Does he share your feelings?" he asks, shutting off the hose and picking up a squeegee to begin work on the windows.

I think back on the things he said last night. The way he said my name. The way he held me when I slept. That funny nickname in Russian that I still don't know the meaning.

"I think he does."

Elijah shrugs. "I don't know a lot about him, but I

know this. Nothing comes out of his mouth that he doesn't mean. I've seen how he watches you when you're not paying him any attention. It's the same way my father watches my mother. I hope someday to have someone who will look at me like that. And what I know from working with you is that you are serious and are self-possessed. I would never doubt your decisions where love is concerned."

I take a step back and guffaw a little too loudly. "Who said anything about love?"

Elijah simply shakes his head and laughs. "I'm happy for you. And if he hurts you, he'll have to deal with me," he says, puffing out his chest.

"Really?"

"Not really; he looks like he could probably kill a man with his thumbs."

I wave off this comment and let Elijah return to his work while I head downstairs to check on breakfast.

When I don't see Maksim right away, I feel a little disappointed. The oven is on, and a heavenly aroma of cinnamon fills the room. There are about half a dozen eggs on the boil, too, and some kind of mouthwatering sauce is bubbling on the stove. But no Maksim. I'm sure he's close by.

A part of me was looking forward to catching him alone.

In the middle of frothing the cream for the guest's coffee, a heavy pair of hands brace my hips. "Good morning, sexy."

Maksim's cool breath against my neck sends shivers down my spine. So that's how it's going to be. Okay. Okay, I like the idea of not walking away from what we just did and pretending it didn't happen.

I push back against him and feel his hard length

already swelling. "Good morning to you. What's for breakfast?"

He hums into my ear and murmurs, "Thought I'd try your ass since we sampled everything else last night."

Heat races down to my core, and I feel my cheeks burn red at the suggestion. I slap his hand. "I meant, what do I tell the primary you're serving for breakfast?"

"Eggs Benedict and—"

A loud gasp drowns out the chef's recitation of the morning menu, followed by Star asking, "What's happening?"

I wait for Maksim to remove his hands from around my waist, back away, retreat into that cool, emotionless professional. Or worse, launch into his frequent complaints about too many crew members in his galley.

But he doesn't do any of that, nor does he shy away from what Star just saw. Keeping his hands on me, he turns us around and says, "She lost a bet. Now she's stuck with me."

Poor Star looks confused as if her brain is buffering. "Here," I say, handing her the captain's favorite coffee mug, with a brew exactly how he likes it first thing in the morning.

She takes it, wide-eyed. "But that's your job. You always bring the captain his coffee in the morning."

I nod in acknowledgment. "And you worked especially hard last night, helping with the party theme. I already chatted with the captain about everything, and he's very pleased with the feedback from the guests. It would be good for you to go up to the bridge and say hi."

"Say hi? And bring him coffee?"

I explain, "The more the captain sees your face in his office for a good reason, the more likely you'll be next in line for a promotion."

"Got it," she says. "Thanks!"

I manage to slip out of Maksim's grip. "I have coffee to deliver to guests, and you have to finish prepping breakfast."

He corners me against the fridge for a playful kiss. He tastes of mint, and his skin smells of soap and pine. Teeth scrape against my neck, and he murmurs, "When are we going back to bed?"

I can't recall ever feeling this wanted by anyone. And not just in a horny way. Just…someone who wants to spend so much time alone with me. It's strangely heartbreaking, in a way.

My hands traveling down his chest, I have to look down, so he doesn't see me making a weird sad-but-happy face. "The guests are going into Naples for some shopping. I could make them a lunch reservation there and buy us some time for a nap."

"Clever girl." He kisses a path up my neck, and once again, my blood heats.

"We'd better hustle with breakfast, for real. There's probably more than just one guest awake and hungry by now," I say half-heartedly, my body blooming with desire with Maksim's teeth and breath on my neck.

His lips, teeth, and tongue blaze a fiery path down to the collar of my uniform polo shirt. I finally gather all my inner strength and stiffen under him. "Later," I say, pushing back against his chest. He heaves a sigh.

"Later," he acquiesces, backing off slowly. I watch him saunter away, then bend over to remove the fresh-baked muffins from the oven. I smile at the view.

I can't wait to skip lunch and take a "nap."

Chapter Nine

Maksim

"WHAT DO YOU MEAN, you don't have a phone?"

And this begins the part where a relationship gets complicated. Juno has asked for my number to add to her phone. As it turns out, she has to accompany our guests on their afternoon away in Naples. The captain wants Star to stay on board to finish laundry and for Juliet to have more experience with cleaning cabins and dinner prep. Apparently, the captain feels that Juno has earned an excursion, and there's no talking him out of it.

"I mean, I do not own a mobile phone. I'm sorry."

Juno's expression is incredulous, and I understand why. I might be the only person on the planet without one. The harbor in Naples is bustling with activity. The guests are already on the dock, where they and the new deckhand Andre are waiting for Juno.

She trains her face into one of sympathy, and I don't like it.

I have to explain certain things about myself, which make zero sense to people with no ties to any criminal underground.

It would be easy to lie, and I might lie if this was simply a boat romance. It would do no harm if this was a no-strings-attached hookup. But this? This is not a no-hard-feelings situation. It will kill me to lie to her. But if I tell the truth, I would scare her away. Any good opinions she may have begun to form about me go out the window.

I don't want to lose what we've started.

"You can radio me. Enjoy your afternoon, and I'll see you at dinner service."

She dares a quick kiss where we stand on the aft deck for everyone to see. I pull her closer for one more kiss, while I hear the guests whistling in approval.

She murmurs against my lips, "The point is, I was going to send you dirty texts. But now you'll just have to imagine me trying on a skimpy new push-up bra."

My body tightens. "Juno," I warn. "I don't have to imagine it. You will wear it tonight at dinner service, and afterward, I will paint your tits with my cum while you wear it."

She gapes at me. "Fuck you for saying that right when I need to leave. I'm gonna be thinking about that all day." Juno shoots me a glare as she whirls around to join the guests.

Chuckling as I watch her go, I find satisfaction at sending her off with a red hue in her cheeks and a wobble in her knees.

Back in the galley, I skip my scheduled nap and begin dinner prep early. Tonight, the guests want a casino night, making everyone's jobs easier. It leaves my menu options wide open, and I intend to wow them with what I can do.

I'm still laughing to myself about how less than 24 hours ago, we were at each other's throats over food.

Fighting with her was delicious, frustrating torment. Giving in to the need for her was easy. Being with her is easy. This thing with Juno has worked its way into me like she belongs there. The banter, the bickering, I realize now, were just the two of us reacting to the way the air crackled between us. Both of us are stubborn and determined as billy goats.

And that's when I realize I could easily fall in love with Juno.

I'm going to have to be very careful. She does not deserve drama.

Instead of distracting me from my job, I feel energized. I pour myself into dinner prep, pulling out all the stops.

Sometime that afternoon, I take a stroll out onto the dock to visit the fishing boats. There, I buy the freshest fish caught just this morning.

Apparently, the universe has a sense of humor. Just as I've planned out the perfect five-course dinner with locally caught fish, I get a radio message that turns everything upside down.

"Maksim, Maksim, Juno."

My body's response to her voice on my radio is Pavlovian. My mouth salivates, and my palms sweat. So much my radio nearly slips out of my hand.

"Copy."

"I hate to do this to you, but the guests have made some friends and asked if they can bring them back to the boat for dinner. I haven't given them an answer yet."

I spit out a curse but then radio back. "Are they listening?"

"They're having drinks, and I just stepped outside so

they can't hear me. It's five people, all men. Do you want me to finesse them? Find a way to redirect?"

Those words remind me of our arguments, and I feel a twinge of regret. I don't want to tell her how to do her job. I want her job to go as smoothly as possible so that I can get to spend more time with her. I want her happy at all costs. I haul ass back to the fishing boats and tell her, "The more, the merrier. We'll make it work."

"Thanks, chef. Your, uh, present is forthcoming."

Chapter Ten

Juno

AFTER DRINKS, the five new friends of the guests treat them to shopping in the fashion district. Here, I duck into a lingerie shop.

While I'm in the dressing room, trying on a racy red number, I smile at how I look in the mirror, noticing the blush to my cheeks, the love bites on my chest. So lovely of Maksim to not leave any marks visible while I'm in uniform.

My body hums at the memory of his mouth, lips, and how he savored every inch of me. The taste of him in my mouth. The way his hands held me, moved me to just the right spot. The way he knew what I wanted, what I needed.

What I need right now is to be alone with him again. Time, we need more time. To work out the kinks, to work out our differences. To fuck me in a private hotel room—not on a boat—until I scream his name.

The words overheard in the Russian accent coming from the dressing room next to mine cause me to freeze. "It is him, the yacht chef. What a birthday surprise, eh?"

The voice, a man's voice, then speaks in all Russian, and I can no longer understand the words.

Silently, I scramble to get dressed. I have to get out of here and tell the captain. If these friends of our charter guests are truly known to the chef, then we need to plan an extra-special surprise for Maksim.

I pay for my bra and panties and wear them out of the store under my clothes; I need to hurry to find a bakery with a cake already made, fast. First, I check in on the guests, browsing and cooing over an open-air stall in the street selling shoes. I let them know that I'm going to duck into a bakery and that I'll check in with them again in a few minutes.

After the cake is sorted, I meet with the guests and their friends, who are all gathered, waiting to be taken back to the yacht by tender, with Andre driving.

As protocol dictates, I take down all their names. Blinking innocently at the one who seems to be the leader, I say, "Are you Russian? It just so happens our chef is Russian," I say.

The leader, named Sergei, winks at me. "You guessed right. I have a confession. We are, of course, charmed by your guest's company, but we have a secret. We had an ulterior motive. We wanted to find our brother, Maksim, and say happy birthday in person."

Excitement flutters in my belly. Nothing makes me happier than provoking that big grump, and now that I know his birthday, tonight will be extra special.

Come hell or high water, Maksim will have some joy after a hellish night of dinner service for 17.

I can't wait to see the look on his face when he sees his brothers.

Chapter Eleven

Maksim

It has been a long time since I've had to cook for this many people.

I had not lied when the captain hired me; I did spend most of my childhood making sure my brothers and sisters had enough to eat. I could make meager amounts of cabbage, rice and beets stretch as far as needed. But it's been a while. And this is not cabbage.

Seventeen hors d'oeuvres plates with cheap caviar are ready to go right at eight p.m.

"Maksim, the guests are seated and ready for the starters."

The galley is a flurry of activity as all the stews and deckhands load their arms with plates and float out into the sky deck. Juno is the last to go and seems to be stalling for a few seconds.

"What is it, malysh?"

"What does that mean?"

My eyes land on her lips, and I say, "Baby."

Her lashes flutter as she looks me up and down like a

five-star cut of meat. "What was that other thing you said earlier?"

"I'll tell you tonight," I promise.

She smiles in a way that tells me she is keeping some secret.

Her eyes travel up and down my body again like I am on display. That's fine. She may look at me like a piece of meat; she makes me feel things I have not felt in ages for anyone.

"Something else? The guests are waiting, my treasure."

Juno's eyes flash, her lips part. She shakes her head no and blinks rapidly, and that's when I see the sparkle of a tear in her eyes. I don't know what I said, whether good or bad.

She's off to deliver her plates before I can study her more. Something is on her mind.

Maybe she's thinking about the pretty new things she purchased today that I haven't yet had the chance to see.

If that's the case, I want this dinner service over as soon as possible. I want the girls to keep the alcohol flowing, so these guests pass out early.

I smile to myself as I chop vegetables and stir the soup. A dark fantasy enters my mind; I could always add a little something to their food to make them sleepy. I'm an expert at making people's evenings end quickly and painlessly. The man I am now would never, ever do that. The man I was before would never hurt an innocent.

My gut clenches when I am reminded that that subject will be a hurdle if I take this connection with Juno much further. Do I tell her tonight? Do I wait until I've fallen in love with her before telling her the truth about my past?

The painful truth is that Juno, and anyone who brings me the slightest happiness, would be safer sharing a life with someone other than me.

When I'm finished chopping vegetables, I realize I've done way more than what is required, even for 17 people.

My skills with a knife are still wired into my muscle memory. Knowing that makes me shudder at things I've done with knives like these before. Sure, these things were done to career criminals, corrupt politicians, the list of bad people, goes on and on. Still, each of their names is written on my soul. Each death sliced off a year from my life.

I shift my focus to the clock, which tells me it's time to start ladling the bisque and take the bread out of the warmer to be sliced.

Juno pops her head back to the galley, looking sheepish. "I am so sorry," she says.

I continue ladling. "What is it? What is wrong, Juno?"

She stammers, "The…the guests' friends are complaining about the cheap caviar."

I come to full height and look at her. "And the primary?"

Juno shrugs. "The primary is fine with what they ordered. Everything is exactly as they had requested on the provision sheet. But the extras, their…friends. I've never encountered this before. They are asking if you have something called…Almas?"

My stomach rolls over at hearing the name of the most expensive and rare caviar in the world. In most countries, it is illegal. Only a particular type of underworld customer is so entitled to think a chef can make that happen. And my former boss, Sergei, is precisely that kind of customer.

I take a deep breath and train my face not to show any emotion. It's just a coincidence.

I nod my head slowly. Calm yourself, Maksim.

Growling, I say, "Tell them that Almas is illegal for me to order. So you know, it is a rare beluga. But I just so happened to have something that should suffice, that I ordered for myself. I was saving it for a special occasion, but I'll get it."

When my back is turned, I hear her say, "What special occasion? Like your birthday?"

I freeze, then turn. "What?" Instantly regretting how cold I sound, I take a step toward her.

"Nothing, nothing. I'm just surprised you actually have some. Never mind, I said nothing. You didn't hear me say anything. I'll let them know you don't have the beluga."

She turns and radios Star, who is still attending to the sky deck, to have her let them know that some kind of exceptional caviar is forthcoming.

How did she know today is my birthday? How? I've told no one.

I plate up the appetizers and slide them onto the metal countertop with trembling hands.

She could not have known because even my personnel file contains a fake birthday. The identity I assumed when I left Moscow was utterly fake, down to the personal taxpayer identification number. The only vestige of my former life was my name, Maksim, a name handed down in my mother's family, one of my middle names.

"Are you feeling ill? Maksim, you're shaking," Juno breathes.

"Go," I order abruptly.

It was a little too curt, a little too loud.

I regret the tone as soon as I see the slight shadow of hurt on her face. She immediately masks the pain with her wry smile and her wit.

"I'm going, I'm going. Try to control yourself when you watch me walk away." She shoots me a dark smile, then sashays out of the galley. That swing of her hips slices through the worry. It's all just a coincidence.

It can't be Sergei. I have to believe it simply cannot be.

Chapter Twelve

Juno

I MIGHT HAVE RUINED the surprise.

And Maksim's mood.

What did I expect?

If I had been thinking, I would have guessed that he wasn't a big fan of birthdays. He may be an egotistical chef, but he is secretive and humble regarding himself, his authentic self.

He is ashamed of his past, his humble beginnings, based on the crumbs that I've managed to pick up.

Maksim needs to understand, he and I are not all that different. We were both dealt unlucky hands, and we both did what we needed to do to survive. He should give himself more credit. He should let himself celebrate good things. Especially the fact that he survived whatever badness life dealt him, and he was granted another year of life. Because we are not promised anything.

I only wish Maksim was not in the galley because this

sunset cruise dinner is spectacular. The captain has cut the engines about a mile south of the harbor of Naples; this is maybe the most spectacular view I've ever seen in my life.

The fact that his brothers are on this ship, just feet away from the galley, is killing me with excitement.

The fact that they don't know that I know who they are is even worse than torture.

I make a mental note never to plan a surprise party for Maksim because I cannot contain myself. I almost blurted it out in the galley a minute ago.

I mentally check myself. Where do I get off, assuming I'm going to be with him on his next birthday? Sure, I think I like him enough that I want to keep exploring this thing between us. I think what we have could continue off this boat, but does he?

We've made no declarations or claims on each other.

It was only your first night, Juno.

It's my heart. I can't help planning for the future. I put so much of my heart and soul into making sure the future for my younger siblings was taken care of; I have a hard time getting out of that headspace.

"What kind of cheese is this?"

My attention snaps back into the present moment when one of the primary's new friends, a large man in a linen suit and Rolex watch, asks about the cheese that Maksim has garnished on top of the tomato bisque.

I paste on the brilliant smile I save for guests. "Caprino fresco: a herbed goat cheese, locally sourced."

The man leans forward, the same man who had requested the illegal caviar. "Ask him if he has any comté... Alexei, what is the name of that cheese?"

"I don't remember, boss, I'm sorry," replies the slightly younger but larger man sitting next to the first.

Boss? Who calls a brother that?

Also, I really don't like how any of these men are staring at me, Juliet, or Star. Likewise, they seem to be sizing up the deckhands.

The hairs on the back of my neck stand on end. Something is not right.

That's when I decide I need a buffer. I need someone to take the edge off this back and forth between me, these men, and Maksim.

I need comic relief. I need someone to distract these men from harassing me while I'm attending to the needs of the actual guests.

I need Captain Joe.

Chapter Thirteen

Maksim

WONDERFUL. Now I have to quickly create a portion of the main course for the captain.

I don't know where Juno is or why she's not radioed me this news that the captain has been asked to join the party. I had to hear it from one of the deckhands.

Cursing, I plate the last portion of sea bass and pray that nobody asks for seconds. If they do, the primary and rest of the paying guests will have to fight over what's left. Nothing for whoever these irritating new friends are.

I have managed to calm myself down in the time between the starters and main. All of it, plus the birthday comment, is just a coincidence. It is a byproduct of my paranoia.

My mind is still on high anxiety; it will take a while before I behave like an average person with normal human reactions to coincidences and inconveniences.

Like right now, my nerves are acting up because I

haven't seen Juno in a while. A preternatural urge to watch over her is hard to manage.

Dessert is coming out of the oven now.

Finally, Juno appears in the galley.

With no one else around for this brief minute, my legs eat up the distance between us, and I back her against the giant whiteboard between the fridge and the entryway.

She gasps, her body rigid against mine when I steal a rough kiss. My tongue sweeps into her warm mouth. Juno sighs softly, arching her back off the whiteboard and grinding her pelvis against mine. God, that feels good. She begins to laugh and taps me gently on the chest.

Against my will, I pull away. "Why didn't you tell me they asked the captain to join them?"

Her cheeks heat, and her focus shifts to someone or something across the room. I turn and see that Captain Joe has walked in on our interlude.

"Because Juno was the one who asked," Joe says. "It seems the extra dinner guests are giving her the creeps. In the meantime, let's try to keep our tongues inside our own mouths, at least while you're on dinner service and guests are waiting for dessert?"

Juno apologizes. "Sorry, Captain. I distracted him."

The captain clears his throat as Juno stands up straighter than usual, smoothing her black uniform dress.

"Anyway," he says. "The primary says she would like to pay compliments to the chef. She and all of the guests are raving about your food. Including their group of new friends, despite them being extra creepy."

I nod, though these formalities embarrass me. "Be right there, Captain."

He shoots me a stern look. "Now. Let's get this over with because I want some of that bread pudding."

Without another word, he exits for the sky deck. The

next second, the rest of the crew swarms in to gather up dessert plates.

Let's get this over with.

Juno goes last, but I insist on carrying three plates, so she only has to take two. She works too hard.

On the sky deck, my entire soul turns to ice. There, sitting across the table from me, wearing a linen suit and looking like a mobster pretending to be on vacation, is Demidov Sergei Kirillovich. The head of the Demidov arm of the Bratva. Sergei.

My body freezes, but I train my face; I cannot let anyone know what's happening.

Sergei looks back at me with a mildly amused expression.

Scanning the table, I set eyes on the rest of his team of underlings. Yvgeney, Misha, Stas, and Alexei. The entire gang from my childhood in Siberia, all of us now overgrown workhorses for the Bratva. They found me. I can't think how, but they did.

I tear my eyes away from Sergei and look at Juno. Her expression is expectant.

The primary, Whitney, stands up and claps. "Compliments to the chef!"

The remaining guests cheer, whistle, and clap, and it takes everything in me to act graciously. Juno's eyes are on me, as are those of the Demidov gang.

Returning her gaze, I try to communicate with her. I need the entire crew off this boat.

My sweet girl looks back at me like there is something deeply wrong with me. My anxiety must be showing.

I bow deeply to the primary, say thank you, and smile as much as possible, which doesn't come naturally to me.

My eyes cut casually over to Sergei. I can't see his hands. I can't see any of their hands. God knows what they've got under the table. They could strike at any second.

What do I do? They say I'm a natural-born killer. I can take down anyone in hand-to-hand combat. One on one, yes. But five guys? No. Five guys who probably have guns when I don't have the element of surprise on my hands? Definitely not.

Maybe I'd have a chance if they'd sent one assassin to take me out. No one can lurk in the shadows and cut me from behind. I'm too quick; I'm smaller than these guys, but far more lethal.

But an ambush in public, with civilians watching?

Fuck my life.

Chapter Fourteen

Juno

WHAT IS WRONG WITH MAKSIM?

Come to think of it, what is wrong with all these guys?

None of them look happy to see each other. And I'd hardly call that evil half-grin on Sergei's face one of brotherly love.

I examine Maksim's face. Yes, he knows the men, but he is not happy to see them.

And I allowed them on the boat. I should have said no. I've never said no to a guest in my life, and that's how I got this far. And now, I'm chief stew, and my own accommodating ways—yet hard-assery with the crew—have come back to bite everyone in the ass.

The captain, to my horror, stands up, rubbing his stomach. "Well, I don't know about you all, but I am absolutely stuffed. I am ready to call it a night."

"Aww, goodnight, Captain," says the primary, Whitney, who goes in for a hug. The captain takes the hug, but discomfort is written all over his face. For a second, it looks as if Star is ready to throw hands. Bless her little heart, she must have a hopeless crush on the captain.

The captain nods to Sergei and says, "Well, as you might not know, according to maritime law, once the captain goes down for the night, any extra guests must exit the boat. The tender will be ready shortly to take you back to shore. Thank you so much for joining us."

I am pretty sure he's making that up. What the hell is Captain Joe doing? I don't get a chance to find out, as he seemingly moseys away to his cabin nonchalantly. Really?

Maksim fidgets with the buttons of his black chef's jacket.

"One last thing, I want to wish my old coworker, Maksim, a happy birthday," Sergei drawls.

Coworker? I thought they were brothers? What the hell is going on?

Everyone freezes. There's a moment of shocked silence, and my mind scrambles. All I hear is the gentle lapping of water against the hull.

Another one of the paying guests then turns to me and slurs, "Hey! How about a birthday kiss for the chef?"

Inwardly I groan, as all eyes are now on me. The guests continue their cheers and claps and whistles, now with added catcalls. This is not how I want to give Maksim a birthday kiss. He looks like he's seen a ghost. But I perform, just like a show horse, as Maksim says. I go to him and lean forward for a kiss. His hand slips around my waist, squeezing my side so tightly that I gasp. We lean into each other and kiss briefly, sweetly, and then I am over-come with the urge to hug him. I don't know what is going on, if it is a full moon, if these people are here to deliver bad news, or what. I want to make it better because he's clearly going through something. During the hug, though, something else happens that sets every hair on the back of my neck standing straight up. Maksim whispers, "Can you be brave for me?"

"Yes, Maksim," I murmur, keeping my face plastered with a congenial smile.

"Muster the guests," he whispers.

My mouth goes dry, and I think I might pee my pants. But of course, I was trained for this. "Done."

The hug ends, and Maksim disappears into the galley with Sergei.

These are probably not his brothers, I finally realize.

I want to break something; I'm so mad at myself for letting whatever is about to happen, happen. I'm so mad at myself for giving these men access to the boat, whoever they are.

And then, I want to kick Maksim's ass for not telling me whatever it is that might have been useful to know. Like why a group of big, heavily tattooed Russian guys who happen to be traveling together might be looking for him.

And then, everything happens in slow motion. My insides turn to solid ice when someone grabs me from behind, something cold and hard pressed against my throat.

Chapter Fifteen

Maksim

As I STARE into the face of my past, my past looks back at me with none of the feigned amusement of minutes ago.

Sergei has cleverly positioned us in the galley so that my back is to the monitors.

"We can do this quickly. Or we can make it painful and slow."

Inside, I seethe. On the outside, I'm as indifferent as an iceberg. "If you want me to beg for my life, you don't know me like you think you do," I tell him coldly.

Sergei's eyes narrow. "Oh. I know you. Brutal and fast. So fucking fast that the Bratva has never seen anything like you before. You are a legend. What are you doing on this rusty bucket? All you had to do was say you wanted to retire. You'd be in a palatial penthouse in Dubai, living out your life, sharing your bed with a different woman every night."

I bristle at the multiple women comment. "I did tell Igor I was retiring, but he wouldn't let me go."

Sergei nods at the comment about his boss, the head of the Demidov family. He glances up at the monitor briefly, his smile spreading. "I understand he only wanted one more job from you."

"You know I couldn't do that job. I said from the beginning. No kids. No women."

Sergei shrugged. "The CIA is breathing down our necks. Igor just wanted to make sure he could trust you with everything you know about him. It would have been so easy."

"Easy," I spit out. "I would rather end my own life than live with the guilt over hurting an innocent."

"The wives and children of the Bratva benefit from the entire system," he replies.

Why am I arguing with this man?

Then, I hear the yacht's horn. I have no idea who made it to the bridge or how, but the emergency message of seven short blasts followed by one long blast echoes across the water.

Without taking my eyes off him, I become aware that the sink behind Sergei is piled high with dishes. The clock on the wall says 11:30 p.m. We should be wrapping up and going to bed by now. I should be in bed with Juno, blanketing her in kisses, telling her the truth. Instead, I was a coward. I wanted to tell her everything. I tried to tell her that I was falling in love with her.

"I would not say anything to anyone. I think my loyalty was never a question before," I say.

Sergei shakes his head. "That is not for me to decide."

He's only here as Igor's lackey. "Sending my former boss to promise me luxuries I do not care for is not the way to convince me of anything."

"Oh, we know." Sergei nods up at the monitor. "We figured out the easier way to get you to comply."

The ice running through my veins turns to fire. There, on the small black and white screen, is Juno. My Juno, and Stas has a knife poised at her jugular.

My blood explodes in my veins. Without turning to face Sergei, I shout my demands to call this off. "Let her go. Tell him to let her go!"

Sergei laughs coldly. "He will. As soon as you agree to come back to work."

I have to think quickly. My breath is fire in my lungs at seeing my girl helpless in the grip of the Bratva. I reach inside the pocket of my chef's jacket.

"Not so fast, brother," Sergei croons, the last word dripping with sarcasm. "Put your hands on the countertop where I can see them."

The flat surface directly in front of me is not, in fact, a countertop but the stainless steel electric cooktop. It's not been used since I made omelets and pancakes this morning, so I know it's cold to the touch.

Unfortunately, I've forgotten that Sergei is far more cold-blooded than I am. He'll kill me without hesitation if I fuck around.

Unfortunately for him, he might be a murderer, but not as quick or as smart as I am.

My roar rents the air in the room. "My hands! Fuck!"

Sergei stammers. "Wh-what? What the fuck did you do, Maksim?"

That split second of confusion is all I need. My elbow strikes Sergei's neck harder than necessary to cause him to stumble backward. I round on him with another blow, this time my fist to the bridge of his nose while my other hand braces his wrist. I pivot sideways and jerk him forward, slamming him against the cooktop.

As Sergei believed my acting a second ago, his immediate reaction is panic as his face lands against the cold steel surface. Enough confusion follows that the grip falters on his pistol, and I wrench it out of his hand.

The old me would not have hesitated to turn the gun on Sergei and end his life right there. The old me had less mercy, no consequences, and nothing to live for but myself.

Once there was a cold void inside me, now there is a ripple of humanity. Not of warmth for this man, but a simple preference to avoid bloodshed if at all possible.

With that thought driving me, and with no small struggle between the two of us, I drag him to the walk-in freezer door, open it, toss him in, and close the door.

The only thought that exists in my head as soon as I click the lock on the door is Juno.

I have to get to her. If anyone has hurt her, I will rain down hell upon their heads.

Chapter Sixteen

Juno

I've been shoved inside a storage bench in the main salon, where the crew stores the less expensive bottles of wine for when guests are too drunk to care what they're drinking.

In the darkness, I feel around for anything I might use as a means to defend myself. But all there is are glass bottles. Not even a screwdriver. This is my fault for running a tight interior and having consequences for anyone not putting things in their proper place. I could really use something sharp.

Also, it's hot in here.

Someone blasts the ship's horn. Who? Who made it to the bridge? I can't be sure, but I hear the emergency alert: seven short blasts followed by one long.

Confidence rushes through me. Someone will come to help us.

"How long are you planning on keeping me in here?" I call out.

My captor, a muscled, young, and bearded member of the group that infiltrated this boat, answers with a put-upon snarl.

"As long as it takes Sergei to finish the job, and as long as it takes the rest of my associates to stop the boat before we reach the harbor, and we take your tender to meet the rest of our party."

I hear the wood creak as my captor sits on top of the bench, right above my head.

This man had not planned on a hostage situation. He's not in charge, and he does not like to be left to supervise prisoners.

Judging by the young, soft face that I glimpsed when I served the table just minutes ago, I'm sure that he doesn't have it in him to hurt me.

These are all assumptions, of course. But I pick up on details, thanks to my years of serving guests of all stripes. When someone acts up, it usually means they're hungry, sleepy, had too much to drink, or not enough.

So that's the angle I have to work on. It's all I have, because of course, he's taken my radio. So I can't even radio the captain right now.

That slender thread of hope is all I have to keep myself alive and have any hope of getting out of this situation.

"Okay," I say. "So, what are you guys? Drug lords? Arms dealers?"

He doesn't answer. It's one of those things. If it weren't, he might have scoffed. Maybe.

Keep asking questions, Juno.

"I mean, probably not drug dealers. I've served plenty of drug kingpins, and their suits are way nicer than yours. No offense."

A soft snort tells me I've hit a nerve.

"Or maybe it was just a more successful drug outfit

than yours. No shame in that; you have to find your niche."

"Stop talking."

Footsteps click across the deck. My first reaction is anger because someone has evidently gone and retrieved their shoes from the shoe bin, and now the teak will be scuffed.

Get it together, Juno. That is not the point.

"The captain is missing, and the bosun says he does not know where the keys to the tender are," says the second person who has just arrived.

"Sergei said to find those keys; they are waiting for us at the drop point to bring them Maksim at midnight. That's in a few minutes."

"Well, then you'd better tell Sergei. He'll know what to do," says my captor.

Grumbling. Disappearing footsteps.

My captor stands up.

"Hey. Bring me back some crab cakes if you're going to the galley."

That's when I hear the struggle, the scraping of feet, and choking sounds. My palms begin to sweat, not knowing what chaos is happening.

And then, the splash.

There's a man overboard, and I don't even know if it's one of the good guys or one of the bad guys.

I have a decision to make. Stay in here and sweat until someone tells me it's okay to come out. Or take a risk and see for myself.

It doesn't take long to make that decision. The over-powering urge to check on the guests, the crew, the captain, and Maksim, makes that decision for me.

The wood creaks as I slowly open the lid, so there goes my attempt at being stealthy. I freeze for a second, and when nothing bad happens, I slide out of the compartment and see…nothing. No people anywhere in the salon.

I creep outside through the sliding door, my heart racing, sure that I'm about to come face to face with my captor.

Turning on one of the emergency spotlights on the deck, I look over the edge, and I realize two things. One, the engines are not thrusting, but they are still on. This means nobody has dropped anchor…which means the deckies have managed to stall these guys or play dumb.

The second thing I realize is I'm looking right down at the man overboard. Except, he's not overboard, exactly. Below me, tied to the yacht, is the tender. And inside the tender is my captor, hogtied. I look right, and there's another one of the men, tied up in the same way, thrashing against his restraints. There are two, three, maybe four men in there.

Who did this?

Is this it? Is this the end?

Whether we're saved or not, I have to attend to my first duty of making sure the guests are safe.

Italian coast guard sirens blare in the distance. A flare goes up in the darkness from the bow of our vessel.

I sprint from one end of the main deck to the other, then rush below deck, where I find my interior crew huddled around the guests in the crew mess, Dustin and Andre guarding the entryways at either end.

I assess everyone's well-being and snap into service mode. "The police are on their way," I tell them. "But everyone should stay put until the police and the coast guard clear the vessel. Tell me if anyone needs anything, and I'll take care of it."

Elijah shakes his head, "I know what you're thinking,

and I won't let you go into that galley, Juno." Everyone is in agreement, but I am adamant.

"Where's the captain?"

The crew tells me no one has seen him since he went to bed after dinner.

"I have to find Maksim. I have to make sure he's okay," I say.

The voice from behind me is low and soft but also menacing.

"You should listen to your crew, Juno. You should have stayed put until you were cleared that the boat was safe."

I whirl around, and my knees buckle.

Chapter Seventeen

Maksim

I'VE GOT HER. Juno is safe in my arms, and I will spend the rest of my life making sure she stays that way.

"Why didn't you stay put until you knew the boat was safe?" I demand.

Her face is a mask of relief, but I can still see the fierceness behind her eyes.

"I couldn't just sit there and do nothing."

I shake my head as I pull her into my arms. "No. I don't suppose you could."

As dawn breaks, I hold Juno's hand as she tells the police in Naples everything she witnessed.

The men waiting at the drop point out to sea got away, which has her worried, but Sergei and the rest of his henchmen are in custody. And Captain Joe apparently hasn't aged a day since he left the Navy SEALs. With the stealth of a hired assassin, the captain single-handedly subdued every one of our captors tonight, except for

Sergei, and tied them up like a present in the tender for the police to pick up.

Juno looks up at me with anxiousness. "Who were those guys? Are they going to come back looking for you?"

I look into her fearful eyes, and I know it's time to tell her everything.

After she's finished giving her statement, we walk from the police station to a nearby bakery that's open early. Perhaps the treat will help make my confession more palatable.

"You know what I'm going to ask you. How many…" She swallows, hesitating. "People did you kill?"

I tell her the number, and her color drains from her face.

She nods but doesn't respond right away but nibbles her fresh-baked sfogliatelle. As the sun rises, I vow that if she accepts me, I will learn how to bake the famed clam-shaped pastry so she can eat as much as she wants.

"I can't justify anything I've done, but I don't take any of it lightly. I was young and needed money to feed my brothers and sisters, so it started with one job only. Then, one job turned into another, and another. It was too easy. I did it without a mess of emotions. They called me "the reaper," and it stuck. But every act of violence took some-thing away from me. Even snuffing out the life of someone who had done terrible things. It eats away at you. That's why I wanted to get out. I wanted to be free. I never wanted to bring someone else into my mess. I never wanted to assume I could have a nice life."

Words fail me.

And then, I start to tremble. It starts in my hands. The hard stone at the center of my stomach has turned into a boulder, and it might break me apart.

Seeing my pathetic state, Juno jumps into action,

always the helper. She grabs my hand and guides me gently but firmly to the nearest bench overlooking the harbor.

She sits down next to me, sets down her pastry, and turns to face me.

"This, all of this, is a lot," she says.

"I'll understand if this is too much for you. If you never want to see me again. I am sure I'm out of a job now that everything has come to light, so the captain will make me disappear from your life without much effort…."

I trail off then because my Juno sits on top of me, straddling me. She cups my face and forces me to look into her eyes.

Her words cover me with a warmth that I do not deserve. "What I'm trying to say to you, Maksim, is yes, it's a lot. But you don't get to tell me what to do. You don't get to bury yourself under my skin and then pull away again without me having a say in it. Now, you have to listen to me. When I was nine years old, my mother ran off with an old flame, and I was left to care for my younger siblings. My dad was a raging alcoholic. We survived and scraped, and I cared for everyone, including him. I did things I'm not proud of. I stole. I transported things for people in my school backpack from one end of Melbourne to the other. I was caught up in the same sort of system. The only difference is the killing never showed up at my door. There's not that much difference between you and me. But here's the thing. I know what I deserve. I deserve a good life, and I deserve happiness. I deserve love, and I love you."

I cinch her in tight to me. "I love you, Juno."

She gives me a heated look. "What happens next?" Juno asks.

"Next? I think we finish the season together if I'm not fired."

"And then?" Something like worry crosses her face, and I don't like it. "We see how it goes?"

Juno bites her lip in uncertainty, but I take both of her hands on my face in mine. I'm determined to make sure she knows this is not just a romance for now, for one summer.

"And after that, I'm with you. Wherever you go, I go."

Juno nods. "Here's something I worry about. This is my career. I love it. I understand why you chose it as a way to hide out and escape. So if this isn't your calling, we need to talk about it because I want you to be happy."

I clench at the thought of ending this career. It might be my only skill outside of…that other thing. "If the captain gives me a good reference, I want to keep doing this. But we do this as a pair," I tell her. "We work together, no matter what, because I have no plans to let you out of my sight ever again."

I believe I feel a shiver of pleasure run through her.

She sighs. "Should we go back to the boat?"

"I don't want to go back to the boat just yet," I murmur, resting my forehead against her sternum. Maybe my favorite spot in the whole world.

The captain has paid for the guests to once again have a day onshore, as long as they promise not to bring any more guests back to the boat with them. Of course, the yachting staffing company offered to refund them their money if they wanted to cancel the rest of the charter. Whitney and her pals did not want that. In fact, they declared that getting "hijacked by Russian pirates" was the most epic vacation story ever.

"We have some time," I say, running my hand up her thigh.

"I'm not ready to go back to the boat yet either," she breathes.

Within ten minutes, we're in a hotel room. We waste no time, having lost the chance for an afternoon delight yesterday. We shuck our clothes immediately and make love in the most enormous, softest bed I've ever seen.

It's not the frisky, playful sex from two nights ago. This is slow, intense, face-to-face. I move slowly in her, but hard and firm, as her body commands it. And I make it last. Over and over, I drive into her core, her wet heat owning me.

"You're mine, pchelka."

"Yes," she gasps.

"Say it," I command, thrusting into her, my fingers digging into the ample flesh of her thighs.

"First, tell me what that means," she says, her eyes shining."

I smile down at her. "It means you're my busy bee."

She laughs, but with the tiniest of tears leaking from her eyes. I tower over her and kiss them away. "Mine."

"I'm yours, Maksim. And you're mine."

I feel her core gripping down around my cock with the word. My favorite word. Mine.

My thumb works over her tight button as I push in, again and again, filling her and pleasing her with everything I have. I watch her break apart in her climax, hoarsely calling out my name.

"Maksim!" My name in her mouth gives me life. My hard-headed, smart-mouthed, stubborn, kind, caring, strong female. Overcome with how beautiful she looks with her back arched and my name on her lips, my own release barrels through me. I spill into her with a shout of pleasure, repeating her name, calling her my baby girl.

"Shit, malysh."

As I carry her to the shower, Juno says something about the stunning view from our room, overlooking the beach. Still, the view between her thighs is the only world wonder I'm interested in.

But first, I take my time washing her hair, massaging her scalp, working the tension out of every muscle, gently and lovingly washing down every inch of my girl.

Soon, I am salivating for her taste.

Juno hums as I spread her open, losing my senses in her heated core.

Her jagged gasps cause a resurgence in my arousal. Tasting her, and listening to her moans, has me hard all over again.

"Maksim," she whimpers, her sweet cunt flexing around my stabbing tongue as I make out with her pussy.

I pull away to meet her gaze, my mouth releasing with an obscene smacking noise. "Yes, Juno?"

"I'm going limp. My legs."

"Say less, my queen."

Without another word, I lower her onto the shower seat and happily kneel in front of her. And then, I go back to work with renewed energy.

I find it unbelievable that I ever thought to push her away.

I'm done with running. I'm done hiding. I'm done being alone. I am home. On the sea, on land, here or anywhere. Anywhere with my busy little bee is home.

Epilogue

Five years later

JUNO

IT WOULD NOT BE Maksim if he didn't push back about the nachos.

"For the love of god, you do not serve nachos on a superyacht," he fusses as the two of us look over the menu for today.

I arch an eyebrow. "Under normal circumstances, you are correct. But the primary wants what the primary wants. She says right here: nachos. Chicken nuggets. And pink cupcakes."

Since we met, Maksim has completed culinary training, and now he thinks every meal has to be five-star.

I hear tiny footsteps running into the galley behind me. I smile, knowing that it's the primary, and she's here to set the chef straight. She knows what he's like.

Maksim's hard face melts as he looks past me.

"Hello, princess," he says.

"Mommy, do I have to wear this life jacket?"

I whirl around to face our little girl, who turns three today. Sure, maybe renting out the private yacht we both work on for our daughter's birthday is a little extreme. But babies only turn three once, and who knows how long we'll have this life. As Maksim and I have learned the hard way, nothing is promised to us.

I squat down in front of her. "What did we talk about?"

She pouts but repeats with reluctance, "That it's the rules."

I smile and kiss her on the forehead. Maksim picks her up in his big arms and carries her over to the counter, and points to the menu. "Now, are you sure this is what you want? I can make anything for you, princess. Chicken piccata. Duck à l'orange, anything."

Sabine wrinkles her nose. "Nachos and nuggets, Daddy."

He heaves a heavy theatrical sigh. "The daughter of the chef wants nachos and nuggets?"

My heart squeezes while watching our daughter place one pudgy, dimpled hand on his scruffy cheek. "Yours are the best," she squeaks, then leans forward and kisses him.

"You learned that from your mother," he chuckles.

Vanessa pops her head into the kitchen. "There's the birthday girl! Time for games, my little bean!" Sabine kicks her legs and squeals, and Maksim hands her off to her auntie Vanessa, who has volunteered to help with the party today. Her husband, Ian, graciously let us use this vessel for free today. Vanessa couldn't stay away from the boats, so Ian had to buy one and hire his own staff. And now, we spend almost every vacation together.

The perk of working on a boat we're also renting is we have access to a decent size cabin at the end of the party. Sabine and her friends have spent all day playing in the water, taking boat rides, and stuffing their faces with party food. The bunch of them are now passed out in the primary suite, and we're right across the hall.

"I think the princess had a good day," Maksim says, pulling me aside as we clean up the galley together. He plants little kisses up and down my neck, pulls open a button with his teeth, and teases my breastbone with his mouth.

I snort. "You never call me princess," I say.

I joke about this, but I know the reason.

He doesn't have to say it, but he does anyway because he knows I like to hear it.

"That's because you are my queen bee," he rumbles against my skin.

He continues kissing and teasing, and soon my nipples are tight and aching. He knows this without even having to look, and in the next second, my shirt is hiked up to my armpits. His rough hands hold them, his lips coaxing my nipples into painfully tight peaks, one after the other.

I hum softly, knowing I'm not going to bring the conversation back to our quarrel earlier over the nachos and nuggets.

We'll probably always get after each other regarding opinions about menus and service. We'll probably never stay in our own lanes.

And that's okay. We've got our own special lane that we've built together.

THE END

. . .

THANK YOU FOR READING WRECKED! If you enjoyed this story, please visit my website at authorabby-knox.com, where you can find lots more titles to read. While there, be sure to sign up for my mailing list to be the first to know about upcoming projects.

Acknowledgments

Many thanks to Anastasia, my friend in Melbourne, for beta reading this story. And, for being an all-around amazing supporter of indie romance.

About the Author

Abby Knox writes feel-good, high-heat romance that she herself would want to read. Readers have described her stories as quirky, sexy, adorable, and hilarious. All of that adds up to Abby's overall goal in life: to be kind and to have fun!

Abby's favorite tropes include: Forced proximity, opposites attract, grumpy/sunshine, age gap, boss/employee, fated mates/insta-love, and more. Abby is heavily influenced by Buffy the Vampire Slayer, Gilmore Girls, and LOST. But don't worry, she won't ever make you suffer like Luke & Lorelai.

If any or all of that connects with you, then you came to the right place.

About the Author

Ingram Content Group UK Ltd.
Milton Keynes UK
UKHW020740070623
423023UK00014B/596

9 798215 440568